that Speak to the Stars

By Joanna Ho

Illustrated by Dung Ho

HARPER

An Imprint of HarperCollinsPublishers

For my agong, who took me on early morning walks up the mountains of Hong Kong.
For Dad, who used to carry me on his shoulders, and for Harv, the Agong who
looks at his grandkids like they're the only answers that matter.—J.H.

To my dad. No matter where I go in life, you're always in my heart.—D.H.

The other day,
when Baba picked me up from school,
I didn't run in for a hug
the way I usually do;

I stared at my toes
where it was safe.
"What's wrong?" Baba asked,
and all my hurt tumbled out.

"Kurt drew a picture
of our friends," I said.
"He pointed at a person
with eyes like two lines
stretched across his face
and told me,
'That one is you.'"

"But it didn't look like me at all."

When we got home,
Baba stood with me in front of a mirror
and said,
"Your eyes rise to the skies and speak to the stars.
    The comets and constellations
        show you their secrets,
            and your eyes can
                foresee the future.

                    Just like mine."

Baba's eyes that rise to the skies and speak to the stars
are filled with all the surprises
he can't wait to give me
throughout the day.
When he lifts me above his head
and cries, "Ready for takeoff!"
before running through the house
like we're headed toward the heavens,
his eyes shine like runway lights
and tell me,

Lift your arms, my son.
You're going to soar above the clouds.

Baba always looks up,
and his eyes are just like Agong's.

Agong's eyes that rise to the skies and speak to the stars
gaze into the distance
   like they're looking at the world
   through lenses of time.
      The voices of ancestors whisper in his ear,
         speaking in lilting languages
         of rice paddies climbing mountains
            like stairways to the sky,

Mazu's miracles
showing mercy from on high,
and mango milk from night markets
lit with bulbs of light.

Agong has an answer
for every question I ask
on our early morning walks,

but when I hug him good night,
he cups my face in his hands
and looks at me
like I am the only answer that matters.

Agong holds the wisdom of generations,
and his eyes are just like Di-Di's.

Di-Di's eyes that rise to the skies and speak to the stars
are closed so long,
 I grow an inch
  waiting for him to wake up.

When Di-Di's eyelids finally flutter open,
I orbit his crib,
　　making funny faces and singing silly songs
　　　　until his laugh grows so big
　　　　　　it spreads up his cheeks
　　　　　　　　and makes his eyes squeeze shut
again.

He looks at me like
I'm the world,
but he is the sun,
filling my days with light.

Di-Di's eyes that rise to the skies and speak to the stars
are just like mine.

My eyes shine like sunlit rays
that break through dark and doubt.
They lift their sights
on paths of flight
that soar above the clouds.

My eyes gaze into space
  and glimpse trails of light
    inviting me into impossibilities.

The comets and constellations
show me their secrets because
I am the emperor
of my own destiny.

I read a brighter future
in the stars
and will fight to make it reality.

My eyes that rise to the skies and speak to the stars are visionary.

They are Baba
and Agong
and Di-Di.
They are me.
And they are powerful.